THE BERENSTAINS'

B

BOOK

THE BERENSTAINS' B BOOK

A Bright & Early Book

RANDOM HOUSE / NEW YORK

Big

brown

Big brown bear

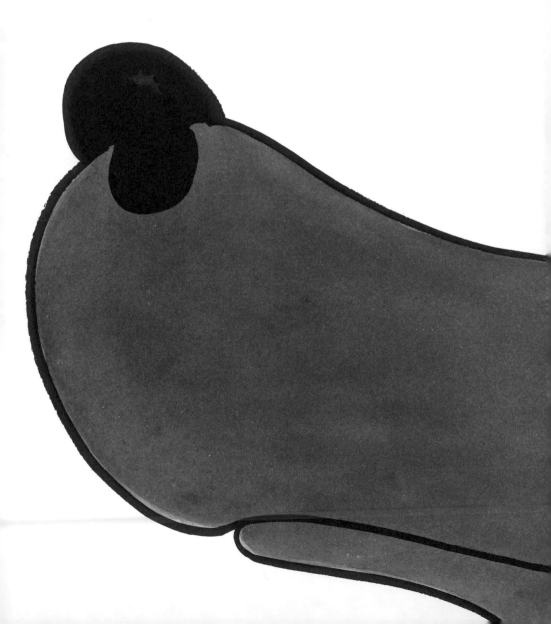

Big brown bear,

blue bull

Big brown bear,

blue bull,

beautiful baboon

Big brown bear,
blue bull,
beautiful baboon
blowing bubbles...

Big brown bear, blue bull,
beautiful baboon
blowing bubbles
biking backward...

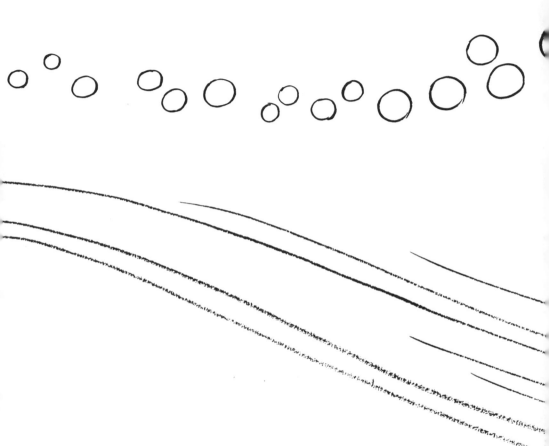

Big brown bear, blue bull,
beautiful baboon
blowing bubbles
biking backward,

bump...

Big brown bear,
blue bull, beautiful baboon
blowing bubbles biking backward,
bump black bug's
banana boxes…

Big brown bear,
blue bull,
beautiful baboon
blowing bubbles
biking backward,
bump black bug's
banana boxes **and**
Billy Bunny's
breadbasket...

Big brown bear,
blue bull,
beautiful
    baboon
blowing bubbles
  biking backward,
    bump
      black bug's
    banana boxes
          and
    Billy Bunny's
        breadbasket
        and...

Brother Bob's

baseball bus...

Big brown bear,
blue bull, beautiful baboon
blowing bubbles biking backward,
bump black bug's banana boxes **and**
Billy Bunny's breadbasket **and**
Brother Bob's baseball bus **and**
Buster Beagle's banjo-
bagpipe-bugle band…

and

that's

what...

broke Baby Bird's balloon.